501 Farm
Things to Spot

igloobooks

Daisy and Colt are the best of friends and love to have fun on the farm together.

Daisy

Colt

See if you can spot them in each picture in this book. Once you've found them, there will be other things to find as well! Let's practice. Can you find Daisy and Colt in the picture opposite?

2 red tractors

3 hen houses

6 pecking hens

Well done! Now you've found Daisy and Colt, see if you can spot these things, too!

Vegetable Patch

Chicken Coop

Daisy and Colt are having an egg-cellent time with their chicken friends. Can you find them hiding in the chicken coop?

Great job! Can you spot these things, too?

1 rooster

3 spades

4 egg-filled nests

7 egg cartons

8 chicks

10 chicken footprints

Big Barn

The farm animals are causing chaos in the barn.
Search every corner and see if you can find Colt
and Daisy hiding among the excitable animals.

Now try and find these things, too.

2 giant tractor wheels

3 ninja chickens

4 hay castles

8 sleeping sheep

9 blue pitchforks

10 slop buckets

Horsing Around

The horses have broken out of their stables and now they're causing havoc with the other farm animals! Can you see where Colt and Daisy are hiding?

**Well done!
Can you spot
these items, too?**

3 cowboy ducks

4 sweeping chickens

6 pig jockeys

7 feed bags   **8 blue saddles**   **10 lucky horseshoes**

Tractor Races

The farm animals are competing in the annual Tractor Championship Rally. Can you see Daisy and Colt? Are they watching the race, or riding in it?

2 chicken umpires

3 cheerleader sheep

5 driving cows

6 pigs with foam gloves

9 gasoline cans

10 checkered flags

On The Duck Pond

Colt and Daisy have taken a trip down to the duck pond for a relaxing afternoon. Can you find Colt and Daisy hiding somewhere around the water?

Good work!
Can you spot
these things, too?

1 fishing chicken

3 diving ducks

4 scuba sheep

6 funny frogs

8 chickens in rubber tubes

10 rowing pigs

Grazing Fields

Daisy and Colt take a shortcut through the flowery meadows,
where the sheep and cows are munching greedily on the grass.
Can you see the two of them hiding in the fields?

Now see if you can find these things.

2 wolves in sheep's clothing

4 black sheep

5 matador chickens

6 plowing pigs

7 prowling foxes

10 milk bottles

Stinky Sty

Colt and Daisy are visiting their pig pals at the yucky, mucky pigsty. Can you find them hiding in the pigsty? Are they keeping clean, or getting muddy?

**Great job!
Can you spot
these things, too?**

2 biohazard chickens

4 pigs in blankets

5 vegetable troughs

6 mud monsters

7 calling roosters

10 muddy T-shirts

Awesome Orchard

Colt and Daisy are feeling a bit hungry, so they wander down to the orchard to find some yummy apples to eat. Find Colt and Daisy hiding among the apple trees.

Now can you spot these things, too?

3 apple bandits

4 apple-filled wagons

5 chickens with ladders

7 jugs of apple juice

8 apple sacks

9 hay bales

Crop Circle Panic

There are some unexpected visitors in the crop field! It looks like the animals are in a bit of a panic. See if you can find Daisy and Colt among the mayhem.

Well done! Now can you find these things, too?

1 friendly alien

3 chicken detectives

4 pigs in UFOs

5 sheep with bouquets

7 mowing horses

10 flocks of geese

Frantic Farmhouse

It's been a long, tiring day on the farm for Daisy and Colt, so they go back to the farmhouse to settle down. See if you can find Daisy and Colt hiding inside the hectic house.

2 ducks in rocking chairs

5 pig farmers

6 cows on beanbags

8 coats of arms

10 log piles

20 bowls of food

Well done!

You spotted everything! Did you find Colt and Daisy, too? Were you looking closely? Can you find these ten things in each picture?

 1 farmer's cat

 1 farmer's dog

 1 funny bunny

 1 red pitchfork

 1 scarecrow

 1 wheelbarrow

 1 ladder

 1 weathervane

 1 vegetable basket

 1 blue bucket

Bonus!

Hidden somewhere within this book is this pinata-hitting horse! Can you spot which picture he is in?